LAKE CLASSICS

Great American
Short Stories III

Alice
DUNBAR-
NELSON

Stories retold by C.D. Buchanan
Illustrated by James Balkovek

LAKE EDUCATION
Belmont, California

LAKE CLASSICS

Great American Short Stories I

Washington Irving, Nathaniel Hawthorne, Mark Twain, Bret Harte, Edgar Allan Poe, Kate Chopin, Willa Cather, Sarah Orne Jewett, Sherwood Anderson, Charles W. Chesnutt

Great American Short Stories II

Herman Melville, Stephen Crane, Ambrose Bierce, Jack London, Edith Wharton, Charlotte Perkins Gilman, Frank R. Stockton, Hamlin Garland, O. Henry, Richard Harding Davis

Great American Short Stories III

Thomas Bailey Aldrich, Irvin S. Cobb, Rebecca Harding Davis, Theodore Dreiser, Alice Dunbar-Nelson, Edna Ferber, Mary Wilkins Freeman, Henry James, Ring Lardner, Wilbur Daniel Steele

Great British and Irish Short Stories

Arthur Conan Doyle, Saki (H. H. Munro), Rudyard Kipling, Katherine Mansfield, Thomas Hardy, E. M. Forster, Robert Louis Stevenson, H. G. Wells, John Galsworthy, James Joyce

Great Short Stories from Around the World

Guy de Maupassant, Anton Chekhov, Leo Tolstoy, Selma Lagerlöf, Alphonse Daudet, Mori Ogwai, Leopoldo Alas, Rabindranath Tagore, Fyodor Dostoevsky, Honoré de Balzac

Cover and Text Designer: Diann Abbott

Library of Congress Catalog Number: 95-76749
ISBN 1-56103-067-8
Printed in the United States of America
1 9 8 7 6 5 4 3 2 1

CONTENTS

❦ Lake Classic Short Stories ❦

"The universe is made of stories, not atoms."
—Muriel Rukeyser

"The story's about you."
—Horace

Everyone loves a good story. It is hard to think of a friendlier introduction to classic literature. For one thing, short stories are *short*—quick to get into and easy to finish. Of all the literary forms, the short story is the least intimidating and the most approachable.

Great literature is an important part of our human heritage. In the belief that this heritage belongs to everyone, *Lake Classic Short Stories* are adapted for today's readers. Lengthy sentences and paragraphs are shortened. Archaic words are replaced. Modern punctuation and spellings are used. Many of the longer stories are abridged. In all the stories, painstaking care has been taken to preserve the author's unique voice.

Lake Classic Short Stories have something for everyone. The hundreds of stories in the collection cover a broad terrain of themes, story types, and styles. Literary merit was a deciding factor in story selection. But no story was included unless it was as enjoyable as it was instructive. And special priority was given to stories that shine light on the human condition.

Each book in the *Lake Classic Short Stories* is devoted to the work of a single author. Little-known stories of merit are included with famous old favorites. Taken as a whole, the collected authors and stories make up a rich and diverse sampler of the story-teller's art.

Lake Classic Short Stories guarantee a great reading experience. Readers who look for common interests, concerns, and experiences are sure to find them. Readers who bring their own gifts of perception and appreciation to the stories will be doubly rewarded.

❦ Alice Dunbar-Nelson ❦
(1875–1935)

About the Author

Alice Dunbar-Nelson began life in New Orleans as Alice Ruth Moore. Her mother, Patricia, was a former Louisiana slave who now worked as a seamstress. Her father was a seaman with a white Creole background. Alice's light skin and red-blonde hair allowed her to get into museums, theaters, and other places that were closed to black Americans.

After college Alice taught school in her home town. She also began to publish poetry and fiction. Many of her stories are set in New Orleans. They describe its varied characters and Creole culture.

In 1898, Alice Ruth Moore married Paul Lawrence Dunbar, the famous black poet. They moved to New York City, where Alice continued teaching. Four years later, the Dunbars divorced.

In 1916, she married Robert J. Nelson, a journalist. She was then teaching at Howard High School in Wilmington, Delaware. Soon she was named head of the school's English Department. She was fired when, against district policy, she attended a political meeting on racial problems.

Alice Dunbar-Nelson was a tireless worker for social and political change. She founded two institutions to help young African-American women: the White Rose Home for girls in Harlem and the Industrial School for Colored Girls in Marshalltown, Delaware. A working woman most of her life, she insisted on the right to be heard. She organized campaigns to win women the right to vote in national elections.

During the 1920s, Dunbar-Nelson edited a newspaper that supported equality for African-Americans. Her columns also appeared in other papers under the titles "From a Woman's Point of View" and "So It Seems to Alice Dunbar-Nelson."

Hope Deferred

Will prejudice put an end to the young man's dreams? Or could it be that hope is stronger than hate?

"WELL, OF COURSE I WANT WAITERS. BUT DO I WANT
COLORED WAITERS? NOW, DO I?"

Hope Deferred

There was no mercy in the blazing August sun. Women wore light dresses. Men mopped the sweat from their faces. The city lay on the borderline between the North and the South.

Edwards joined the perspiring mob on the hot streets. He mopped his face along with the rest. His shoes were dusty, his collar wilted. He caught a glimpse of himself in a shop window. He smiled grimly and muttered to himself. "I hardly look like a man about to present himself before one of the Lords of Creation to ask for an interview."

Edwards was young. He had not yet outgrown his ideals. He had even chosen someone to share them. He had found a woman willing to face poverty with him—for the sake of his ideals. He knew that she was a treasure far above rubies. But ideals do not always supply the things a body needs. It was pure need that drove Edwards into the August sunshine that day.

The man in the office looked up from his desk. His cold gray eyes fixed on Edwards with an impatient stare. He spoke in a thin, icy voice.

"Sorry, Mr.—er—, but I won't be able to grant your request." Then the man gave Edwards a curt "Good morning" and walked out of the room.

"Now what?" Edwards asked himself. He had looked for a job *everywhere*. Now he felt the door of hope closing for good. He wearily dragged himself down the little side streets that led home.

When Margaret met him at the door, both of their faces lit up. There was a glow that always shone when they were together. She quickly drew him into the little room. Her eyes asked what had happened, though her lips did not frame the question. "No hope," he replied to her unspoken question. She sat down suddenly.

"If I could only just stick it out, little girl," he said. "But we need food and clothes. Only money buys those things, you know."

"Perhaps it would have been better if we hadn't married—" she suggested timidly.

"Because you've had enough of poverty?" he asked.

She stood up and put her arms around his neck. "You know better than that. But if you didn't have me, you could live on less. You'd have a better chance to hold out until they see your worth."

"I'm afraid they never will," he said.

He tried to keep his tones even, but his voice shook in spite of himself. "The man I saw today was my last hope. He's the chief clerk. What he says controls the opinions of others. If only I could have gotten past him! Then I might have convinced the senior member of the firm. But he's a man who leaves details to others. Mr. Hanan, the clerk I saw today, was suspicious of me from the first. He thinks I'm either a fraud or an escaped lunatic."

"We can wait," she said softly. "Your chance will come." She soothed him with a sweet smile.

A pile of unpaid bills came in the afternoon mail. They drove Edwards out into the hot sun again. In the past four months he had come to know the main street from end to end.

The usual idle crowd stood around outside the newspaper office. The scores of the day's baseball games were posted in the window. Edwards joined them. "I can be a sidewalk fan, even if I am broke," he smiled to himself. Then a voice at his side said, "See *that!*"

"That" was a brief news item above the baseball scores. As he read it, Edwards got an idea.

STRIKE SPREADS TO OUR CITY
Waiters at Adams' Restaurant
Walk Out After Breakfast Today

"Good!" Edwards said aloud. Then he hurried down the street. For the first time that day he walked with a light spring in his step.

The owner of Adams' Restaurant was thin and wiry. He looked liked a man from a foreign country.

"Of course I want waiters," he replied to Edwards' question. Then he squinted closely at the tall young man. "But do I want *colored* waiters? Now, do I?"

"It seems to me you don't have much choice," said Edwards good-humoredly.

That bold reply seemed to amuse the restaurant keeper. He slapped the younger man on the back.

"I guess I'll try you as head waiter," the man said. Even after the disaster of the morning's strike, he seemed to be in a pleasant mood. "Peel off your jacket and go to work, then. But before that, tell me your name."

"Louis Edwards."

"Uh huh. Had any experience?"

"Yes, some years ago, that is. When I was in school."

"Uh huh. Then waiting tables ain't your general work?"

"No."

"Uh huh. Well, what do you do for a living, then?"

"I'm a civil engineer."

One of Adams' eyebrows shot up.

"Well, say man, you're an *engineer*! What do you want to be strike-breaking here in a waiter's coat for, eh?"

Edwards' face fell, and he shrugged his

shoulders. "They don't need me, I guess," he replied briefly. It was an effort, and the restaurant keeper saw it. But his wonder overcame his sympathy.

"They don't need you with all that going on at the Monarch works? Why, man, I'd of thought every engineer this side of hell would be needed out there."

"So did I. That's why I came here."

"Say, kid. I'm sorry for you. I surely am. You go on to work now."

Edwards told his wife all about it that night. "And so," he said, "that's how I became the head waiter—and also the first assistant."

Margaret was silent. How bitter for him! His lifelong hopes were vanishing. She said nothing, but the pressure of her slim brown hand in his meant more than words to both of them.

"It's hard to keep the vision true," he said quietly.

But if it was hard that night, it grew even more so within the next few weeks.

The striking waiters hung around the restaurant. They were often ugly and threatening. But Adams vowed to keep his restaurant open no matter what.

Edwards was the force that held the replacement waiters together. He used every argument he could think of to keep them all working. But none of his arguments counted as much as the fact that he stuck through all the trouble himself. Some days he wiped off mud that was thrown in his face. Some days he picked up the rotten vegetables that were thrown at the door. Always he blocked the doors at night. More than once he replaced food deliveries that were destroyed by well-aimed stones. He stood close by Adams' side when the fight threatened to grow serious.

Adams was grateful. "Say, kid, I don't know what I'd of done without you," the man said one afternoon. "Now that's the truth. Take it from me, when you need a friend—I'm right there for you." Just that morning the police had arrested some of the most disturbing offenders. These men, by the way, had never worked for Adams. But union sympathy had taken over the town by now.

The humid August days slowly melted into September. The striking waiters had quieted down. Edwards had slowly come to accept his temporary discomforts. Every day he would explain to Margaret that it was only for a little while. Just until he could earn enough to allow them to get away. One day he would be able to stand up proudly in some other place. Then she would see that all his training had not been in vain.

One noisy Saturday night a customer moved towards his table. Edwards recognized the half-sneering face of his old hope. It was Hanan, the chief clerk who had turned him down for a job. To Hanan, the man who brought his food was but one of the many servants who satisfied his daily wants. He had not even looked at the waiter's face. For this Edwards was grateful. Then loud shouting from the streets attracted Hanan's attention. He looked up.

"What are they saying?" he asked. Edwards did not answer. He was so familiar with the threats and jeers that he thought it was unnecessary.

"Yah! Yah! Old Adams hires blacks! Hires blacks!" the cry continued.

Hanan looked up at Edwards' dark face for the first time. "Why, that is so," he said. "This is quite unusual for Adams' place. How did it happen?"

"We are strike-breakers," Edwards replied quietly. Then he felt a flash of uneasiness. A hint of recognition had come into Hanan's eyes.

"Oh, yes. I see," Hanan said. "Aren't you the young man who asked me for an engineer's job not long ago? Weren't you trying to get on at the Monarch works?"

Edward bowed. He could not answer. Hurt pride surged up within him. The rush of feeling made his eyes hot and his hands clammy.

"Well, er—I'm glad you've found a place to work. Very sensible of you, I'd say. Surely you're more fitted for this than you are for engineering."

Edwards started to answer, but the hot words were checked on his lips. The shouting outside had reached a more threatening level. A stone smashed through the glass of the long window. Flying glass struck Edwards' hand and knocked over the dishes on the tray he was holding. Hot food spilled on Hanan's lap. The man sprang to his feet and turned angrily upon Edwards.

"That is criminally careless of you!" he shouted. "You could have prevented that. You're not even a good waiter—much less an engineer."

Then something snapped in Edwards's brain. The long strain of the fruitless summer had worn him down. And now there was this last insult. Suddenly, all of it came together in a blinding flash. Reason and intelligence were put aside. Edwards felt only a mad hatred—and a desire to avenge his wrongs on this man. He sprang at the white man's throat and pulled him to the floor. They wrestled and fought each other in the clutter of overturned chairs and tables.

* * *

The telephone rang over and over again. Adams wiped his hands on a towel. He carefully moved a paintbrush out of the way. Then he went to his desk and picked up the receiver.

"Hello! Yes, this is Adams, the restaurant keeper. Who? Uh huh. He wants to know if I'll put up his bail? Of course not—let him serve his time. I never had no fight in my place before. No, I don't ever want to see him again."

He hung up the receiver and went back to his painting. He had almost finished his sign.

WAITERS WANTED.
ONLY WHITE MEN NEED APPLY.

Out in the county jail Edwards sat on his cot. His head was buried in his hands. He wondered what Margaret was doing all this long hot Sunday afternoon. He wondered if lonely tears were blinding her sight as they were his. Then the warden called his name. Margaret stood before him, her arms outstretched.

"Margaret! Are you really here—in this place?"

"Aren't *you* here?" she smiled bravely. Then she drew him toward her. "Did you imagine I wouldn't come to see you?"

"To think that I've brought you to this!" he moaned.

She listened as he told her the story of what had happened. Then she asked quietly, "How long will you be here?"

"A long time, dearest—and you?"

"Well, I can go home and work," she answered. "I'll wait for you whether it's ten months or ten years—and then—?"

"And then—" They stared into each other's eyes like frightened children. But then his back straightened. The vision of his ideal now lit up his face. He looked at his wife with hope and happiness.

"And then, Beloved, we will start all over again," he said in a strong voice. "Somewhere I am needed. Somewhere in this world dark-skinned men like me are *wanted*. They need me to dig and blast, and build bridges and make straight the roads of the world. I am going to find that place—with you."

She smiled back trustfully at him. "Only keep true to your ideal, dearest," she whispered. "Then you will be sure to find your place. Look, Louis! Your window faces south.

"Look out of it all the while you are here. For it is there, in your own southland, that your dream will become real."

꒰ꈁꔵꈁ꒱

Titee

Little Titee won't mind his parents or his teacher. But he's not really a bad boy. If he didn't have a good heart, he wouldn't have taken on his secret mission.

"AH, WHY DON'T YOUR MOTHER SEND YOU SOME LUNCH
FOR A CHANGE?"

Titee

It was especially cold that day. The sharp north wind bent everything in its track. The usually quiet street was more than empty. It was dismal.

Titee leaned against one of the brown freight cars for protection. He warmed his little chapped hands over a small fire. "Maybe it will snow," he muttered.

It was Saturday, or Titee would have been in school. He went to the big yellow school on Marigny Street. Every day he was happy to be there—not to gain knowledge, but to think of ways to make his teacher's life a burden.

He was a lazy, dirty, troublesome boy, his teacher often said. And he didn't improve as time wore on. Last year he was not promoted to the next grade.

Titee liked a practical joke more than a practical problem. To him, a good game was far more entertaining than a language lesson. Also, he was always hungry. It was his habit to eat in school before the half-past-ten recess.

But there was almost nothing about natural history that Titee did not know. He could dissect a butterfly or a mosquito hawk. He could describe their parts as well as a medical student. The entire Third District was an open book to Titee. That part of the city was filled with swamps and canals and railroad sections—and wondrous, crooked streets. There wasn't a corner he didn't know.

And Titee knew all the gossip. He knew just when the crawfish would be plentiful in the canals. He knew when a poor fellow might get a job in the fertilizer factory. And then there was the levee! There was nothing he couldn't tell you about the ships and sailors.

Titee himself had been down to the Gulf of Mexico. He had been out on its dangerous waters. He had gone out on a fishing boat with some jolly brown sailors. If he chose, he could interest the whole class in that story.

Titee shivered as the wind swept by. He huddled by some freight cars. His cotton coat was very thin.

"Oh, I do wish it was summer," he murmured. He cast a sailor's glance up at the sky. "Don't believe I like snow. It's too wet and cold." He warmed his hands at the little fire one more time. Then he plunged his hands in his pockets and gritted his teeth. Manfully, he started off on his mission. Out across railroad track he went, heading toward the swamps.

It was late when Titee got home. He had performed his errand poorly, and his mother beat him. She sent him to bed without supper. Poor little Titee! A sharp strap stings in cold weather. And a long walk in a biting wind creates a strong appetite. The boy cried himself to sleep that night. But he was up bright and early the next morning. At dawn he went to Mass. He was home before the rest of the family got out of bed.

Something was weighing on Titee's mind. He hardly ate his breakfast. He quickly left the table, cramming the remainder of his meal in his pockets.

"My goodness, what is he up to now?" his mother wondered. She watched his little form trudging away in the wind. His head was bent low. His hands were thrust deep in his bulging pockets.

"Must be a new play-toy on his mind," sighed his father. "He is one funny child."

The next day Titee was late for school. This was unusual. He was always the first one there, working out some plan to make the teacher miserable. Now the teacher looked disapprovingly at him. But Titee made up for his tardiness by being good all day. And he did not even eat once before noon. This had never happened before in the entire history of his school life.

When the lunch hour came, one of the boys found Titee standing by a post. He was unhappily watching a big ham sandwich. It was rapidly disappearing down the throat of a sturdy boy.

"Hello, Titee," the boy said. "What you got fer lunch?"

"Nothin'," was the mournful reply.

"Ah, why don't your mother send you some lunch, fer a change? You don't ever have nothin' to eat."

"I didn't want nothing to eat today," said Titee, blazing up.

"You did, too!"

"I tell you I didn't!" Titee shouted. Then his hard little fist landed on his classmate's eye.

A fight in the schoolyard! Poor Titee

was in disgrace again. He got a scolding from the principal. At home Titee barely could sit still through dinner. Then he was off down the railroad track. His pockets were stuffed with the remains of the skimpy meal.

The next day Titee was late for school again. Again he had no lunch. And the next day as well. The teacher sent a note to his mother. If Titee had not torn it up, it might have done some good.

One day torrents of rain came down from a miserable, angry sky. It was too wet and cold for small boys to be going off to school, thought Titee's mother. So she kept him at home to watch the weather through the window. All day he fretted and fumed like a tiny version of the storm outside. Many times he tried to slip away but his mother caught him.

Dinner came and went. The wet gray sky deepened into the blackness of coming night. Someone called Titee to go to bed. But he was nowhere to be found.

They searched under the beds, and in closets and corners. But he was gone as surely as if he had been spirited away. The neighbors said they hadn't seen him. There was nothing to do but go to the railroad track. Titee had often been seen there, trudging along in the shrill north wind.

With lanterns and sticks, and Titee's little yellow dog Tiger, the search party started down the track. The rain had now stopped, but the wind blew a gale. Great gray clouds scurried over a fierce sky. It was not exactly dark, even though there was neither gas nor electricity in this part of the city. On such a night as this neither moon nor stars dared show their faces. But a kind of glow was in the air. It was as though the atmosphere were charged with an unearthly light.

Titee's family looked everywhere. But they found no signs of the missing boy. The soft earth between the railroad ties crumbled under their feet. But it showed no small tracks or footprints.

"We may as well go home," said Titee's big brother at last. "He's not here."

"Oh, my God," urged the mother, "he is, *he is*. I know it."

So on they went, slipping on the wet earth, stumbling over the loose rocks. Suddenly a wild yelp from Tiger brought them to a standstill. The dog had rushed ahead of them. His barking became a terrible howling.

With new energy the muddy little party hurried forward. Tiger's yelps were getting louder and louder. Now they seemed to be mixed with a muffled wail.

After a while they found a pitiful little heap of sodden rags, lying by the track. It was Titee—with a broken leg. He was wet and miserable and moaning.

His brothers tried to pick him up tenderly to carry him home. But the little boy cried and clung to his mother. He begged not to go.

"Ah, my poor child. He has the fever!"

wailed the boy's mother.

"No, no, it's my old man!" sobbed Titee. "He's hungry!" He pulled a little package out of his coat. It was the remains of his dinner, crumbled and rain washed.

"What old man?" asked the mother.

"*My* old man. Oh, please, I must see him. Don't take me home now."

So, giving in to his wishes, they carried him where he wanted to go. He pointed them up to a levee by the canal. There the big brothers suddenly stopped.

"Why, it's a cave!" one of them exclaimed. "Is it Robinson Crusoe?"

"It's my old man's cave," cried Titee. "Oh, please hurry! We have to hurry. Maybe he's dead."

They went in. The light of their lantern shone on a rumpled bed of straw and paper. On it lay a withered, white-bearded old man. His eyes were wide and frightened. In the corner was a sorry-looking cow.

"This is my old man," cried Titee,

joyfully. "Oh, please, grandpa, I'm sorry I couldn't get here today. It rained all mornin'. And when I ran away, I fell down and broke something. Oh, grandpa, I'm hurt. I'm sorry you're hungry."

So this was the secret of Titee's trips down the railroad track! In one of his walks around the swampland, he had discovered the old man. The poor old fellow was exhausted from cold and hunger. He had become sick. Together they had found this cave. Titee had made his bed of straw and paper.

Then one day a stray cow, old too, had crept in. She stayed to share the damp dwelling. This is where Titee had trudged twice a day. For weeks he had carried his lunch there in the morning and his dinner in the afternoon.

The case was referred to an officer of charity. "There's a crown in heaven for that child," the city officer said. But as for Titee—when the leg was well, he went his way just as before.

The Stones of
the Village

Why would a successful
man have such bitterness in
his heart? This is the story
of a man who has it all—as
long as no one discovers his
secret.

"WHY YOU WANT TO PLAY WID DEM BOYS, EH? DEY DON'T CARE FOR YOU. DEY FOOLS!"

The Stones of the Village

Victor Grabert walked down the one wide, tree-shaded street of the village. His heart was aching with bitterness and anger. By now these feelings seemed nearly second nature to him. Now and then his anger flamed out into almost a murderous rage. Shouts of laughter floated in the air behind him. Boys his own age called out names and insults.

At last Victor reached the tumble-down cottage at the far end of the street. He flung himself on the battered step. Grandmere Grabert sat rocking back and forth. She was crooning a bit of song brought over from the West Indies. That was where she'd been born and raised many years ago.

"Eh, Victor?" she asked. That was all she said, but he understood what she meant. He raised his head and pointed a shaking finger down the street.

"Dose boys," he gulped.

Grandmere Grabert laid an old, sympathetic hand on his black curls. But she withdrew it in the next instant.

"Well," she said angrily. "Why do you go by dem, eh? Why not keep to yourself? Dey don't want you. Dey don't care for you. H'ain't you got no sense?"

"Oh, but Grandmere," he wailed. "I want to play."

The old woman stood up in the doorway. Her tall, spare form towered over him.

"You want to play, eh? Why? You don't need to play. Dose boys," she said with a magnificent gesture pointing down the street. "Dey fools!"

"If I could play wid—" Victor began. But his grandmother caught him by the wrist and gave him a little shake.

"Hush!" she cried. "You mus' be goin' crazy." Still holding him by the wrist, she pulled him indoors.

It was a two-room house. Inside it was bare and poor and miserable. Their supper was simple, and they ate it in silence. Afterwards Victor threw himself on his cot in the corner of the kitchen. Grandmere Grabert thought he was asleep. She closed the door and went into her own room. But the boy was awake. His mind was filled with painful events and heartaches.

Victor was thinking that most of his 14 years had been nothing but misery. He had never known a mother's love. His mother had died when he was just a few months old. No one had ever spoken to him about a father.

His Grandmere Grabert had been

everything to him. She was kind, in her stern, demanding way. She provided for him as best she could. He had picked up a little education at the local school. It was a good school. But his life there had been so unhappy that one day he simply refused to go anymore.

Victor's earliest memories revolved around this poor little cottage. He could see himself toddling about its broken steps. He played alone with a few broken pieces of china, imagining they were glorious toys. He remembered his first whipping, too. One day he had grown tired of the loneliness. So he had toddled out after a merry group of little black boys his own age. Grandmere Grabert came to look for him. She found him sitting happily in the center of the group in the dusty street. Grandmere snatched at him fiercely. He whimpered in confusion. For the first time he was learning what fear was.

"What you mean?" she hissed at him.

"What you mean playing in de street wid dose black children?" And then she struck at him wildly with her open hand.

Frozen in shock, he looked up into her brown face. It was crowned with curly black hair streaked with gray. He was too frightened to question her anger.

Ever since that day Victor's life had been lonely. The parents of the little black boys resented Grandmere's insult to their children. They ordered them to have nothing to do with Victor. But when he toddled after some other boys—whose faces were white like his own—they ran him off. He couldn't understand it.

But the hardest thing was when Grandmere made him stop speaking their soft Creole language. It was a part of their shared heritage that held them together. But she forced him to learn English. The result was a confused jumble of words that were no language at all. When he tried to speak it in the streets or in the school, all the boys, both white and black, hooted at him.

Victor tossed and turned on his cot long into the night. He relived all the heartaches of his years. Hot tears burned his face.

The next morning, Grandmere noticed his heavy swollen eyes. A wave of tenderness passed over her. As she served his breakfast, she was gentle toward him. During the night she, too, had been thinking over the matter. Now she had a plan.

* * *

A few weeks later, Victor found himself in New Orleans. He timidly rang the doorbell of a little house on Hospital Street. His heart throbbed with anxiety. What would old Madame Guichard, Grandmere's one friend in the city, be like? Would she be kind to him? He had walked all the way here from the river landing. Now he was hungry and tired.

Never before in all his life had he seen

so many people. It had been a long journey. He had come down the Red River, and then the Mississippi. If it was an interesting trip, Victor didn't know it. He was too sad about leaving home.

Madame Guichard did turn out to be kind, however. She welcomed him warmly. Soon the two of them became firm friends.

Victor had to find work. After all, Grandmere had sent him to New Orleans to "make a man of himself." So Victor felt a responsibility to do just that. He tried to begin his job search bravely.

One day he saw a sign in an old bookstore on Royal Street. In both French and English it stated that a boy was needed. Almost before he knew it, he had entered the shop. With a great effort he choked out a few words to the old man behind the counter.

Over his glasses, the old man looked sharply at the boy.

"Eh, what you say?" he asked.

"I—I want a place to work," the boy stammered again.

"Eh, you do? Well, can you read?"

"Yes, sir," replied Victor.

The old man got down from his stool. He came out from behind the counter. Then he put his finger under the boy's chin and stared hard into his face. Victor's clear, honest eyes met his own.

"Do you know where you live, eh?"

"On Hospital Street," said Victor.

"Very well," grunted the book-seller. He gave Victor a few directions about his work. Then he settled himself on his stool again and went back to his book.

Thus began Victor's working life. It was an easy one. At seven o'clock, he opened the shutters of the little shop, swept the floor, and dusted. At eight o'clock, the book-seller came downstairs and went out to get his coffee. At eight o'clock in the evening the shop was closed again. That was all.

Sometimes, but not very often, a

customer came in. Sometimes there was an errand to do.

In that way a year went by, then two and three. Victor grew tall and thin. Like the old book-seller, he sat day after day poring over some dusty book. He grew pale from so much reading. His mind was filled with a tangled jumble of odd ideas. He made few friends.

Every week, he wrote a letter to Grandmere Grabert and sent her part of his earnings. In his own way he was happy enough with the life he was living. If he was lonely, he no longer cared. His world was full of people and images from the books he read.

Then all at once his safe little world came tumbling down. The old book-seller died one night. His shop and its books were sold. Victor wept as he saw some of his favorite books carried away by strangers. He was sure they could not appreciate their value.

But the next day, he dried his tears. A

lawyer named Buckley came to the little house on Hospital Street. He told Victor that the book-seller had left him a sum of money.

"There's enough money for you to live on," the lawyer told the boy. "It was my client's wish that you should enter Tulane College. He wanted you to study for a profession. He had great confidence in your ability."

"Tulane College!" Victor cried out. "Why—why—why—" Then he suddenly stopped speaking. The lawyer knew nothing about him. So why tell him? "Why—why—I should have to study in order to enter there," Victor said weakly.

"Exactly so," said Mr. Buckley. "I will see to that."

Victor thanked Mr. Buckley and said good-bye. After the lawyer left, the boy gazed blankly at the wall. Then he wrote a long letter to Grandmere.

On Mr. Buckley's advice, Victor soon entered a preparatory school for Tulane.

Mr. Buckley had never bothered to meet Madame Guichard.

* * *

Some years later, lawyer Victor Grabert sat in a handsome office on Carondolet Street. His day's work was done. He leaned back in his chair, smiled, and looked out of the window. Outside, the wind howled. Gusty rains beat against the window pane.

Lawyer Grabert smiled again. He found himself half-pitying those who were forced to brave the storm on foot. In a while he got up, put on his overcoat, and called a cab. His home was in the best part of the city. There he found his old-time college friend waiting for him.

"I thought you were never coming, old man," was his friend's greeting.

Grabert laughed. "Well, I was a bit tired," he answered. "I wanted to relax."

His friend Vannier patted Grabert's shoulder. "That was a mighty effort you made today," he said. "I'm proud of you."

"Thank you," replied Grabert.

"Are you going to the Charles' dance tonight?" asked Vannier.

"I don't believe I will, Vannier. For some reason, I'm feeling lazy."

"Oh, come on! It will do you good."

"No, old man. I want to read and think," Grabert said.

"To think over your good fortune of today?" Vannier asked.

"If you put it that way, yes."

But it was not simply that day's good fortune that Grabert wanted to think about. It was his good fortune of the past 15 years. He had gone from prep school to college, and from college to law school. Now he was a successful young lawyer. His small fortune, which Mr. Buckley had invested for him, had almost doubled. His school career had been pleasant and profitable. He had made friends. Now and then the Buckleys asked him to dinner or invited him to their box at the opera.

Grabert was rapidly becoming a social favorite. All the girls wanted to dance with him. No one had asked any questions about his past, and he volunteered no information. Vannier had known him at prep school. He had told everyone that Grabert was a young country fellow with some money but no connections. He said that Mr. Buckley was his guardian.

Young Vannier's family was socially important and Grabert's personality was pleasing. So Victor easily passed through the doors of the social world and into the inner circle.

One summer, he and Vannier were traveling in Switzerland. A letter came to Grabert at the hotel. It was from the priest of his old home town. The letter said that Grandmere Grabert had died.

"Poor Grandmere," sighed Victor. "She did care for me. I'll go take a look at her grave when I go back."

He did not go, however. When he returned to Louisiana, he was too busy. Finally he decided that it would be useless to go. He certainly had no love for the old village. And he had long ago erased Mrs. Guichard from his list of friends.

Yet, whenever he thought about his many triumphs, he always had a small feeling of annoyance. That uneasy feeling seemed to cast a shadow on every pleasant memory.

"I wonder what's the matter with me?" he asked himself.

He remembered an event from the day before. In court he had seen a well-dressed black man treated rudely by the recorder. Victor had tingled with rage. But why? It was not *he* who had been insulted. "What would have happened if Recorder Grant had any reason to think that *I* was in any way like that man?" he wondered bitterly. "I know he would have treated me no better."

He thought it over for a while, calling himself a sentimental fool. "But what have I to do with *them*?" he asked himself. "I just have to be careful."

The next week he fired the black man who took care of his office. Victor had begun to feel a growing sympathy toward the fellow. Since the event in the courtroom, he was afraid that something in his manner would give him away.

The Vanniers were always interested in Grabert's life—especially Elise Vannier. Victor liked to come by in the evening and talk over his cases with her. He found himself carrying around a faded rose which she had worn. Once he started to throw it away, but suddenly kissed it instead. Now he kept it in his pocketbook. He could easily see that Elise liked him. And then one evening, when they were talking, the conversation drifted to summer plans.

"Papa wants to go to the country house," said Elise. "Mama and I don't want to go. It is so dull out in the country! Don't you think so?"

Victor recalled a pleasant visit there and laughed. "Not if you are there."

"If you'll promise to come visit me sometimes, it will be better," she said.

"If I may, dear Elise, I should of course be delighted to come."

Elise laughed. *"If you may,"* she teased. "Oh, but Victor, don't you have a country home of your own somewhere? It seems to me that Steve mentioned it years ago. I wondered that you never spoke of it."

Victor felt cold sweat on his brow, but he managed to answer quietly. "No, I have no home in the country."

"Well, didn't you or your family *ever* own one?" Elsie asked.

"Oh, that was an old place a good many years ago," he replied. A vision of the little old hut with its tumble-down steps flashed in his mind.

"Where was it?" Elise asked.

"Oh, way up in St. Landry—too far

from civilization to mention," he said quickly. Elise was too deep in her own thoughts to notice his hollow laugh.

"And you don't have a single living relative?" she continued.

"Not one," he said.

"How strange," she said. "Why, I have dozens of cousins and uncles and aunts. Without them I would feel out of touch with the world."

He didn't reply, and she chattered away about something else.

That night in his room, he paced the floor. "What did she mean?" he asked himself. Did she suspect anything? Then he dismissed the thought. If Elise really wanted to find out about his background, she would ask him directly.

He must prepare himself to answer questions. The family would want to know all about him—if he were going to marry her. But *was* he going to marry Elise? That was the question.

Well, he thought, *why not*? What was

the difference between him and the other suitors who courted her? They had money—and so had he. They had an education, polite training, culture, social position. And so had he. But they had family traditions, and he had none.

Anyway, Elise loved him. He had only to look into her eyes and read her soul to know that was true. Perhaps she wondered why he had not spoken. *Should* he speak? There he was, back at the old question again.

"According to the standard of the world," he thought, "my blood is tainted. It's not pure. But who knows it? No one but myself, and I shall never tell. In all other ways, I am quite as good as the rest. And I'm the one Elise loves."

But even this thought quickly lost its sweetness. Elise loved him because she did not know. Now he found rage and disgust rising in his heart. His anger burned at these people whose prejudices made him live a life of lies.

Well, he would simply stop worrying about their traditions! He would be honest. But immediately he found himself fearfully shrinking in fear from that possibility.

It was the same old problem that he had faced in the village. In his imagination the boys, both white and black, were running after him again. Still they held stones in their hands, ready to hurl them at him.

Sleep was impossible. He rolled and tossed miserably. Until now he had thought little about the subject. He had drifted with the tide and accepted what came to him. It seemed the world *owed* him his good fortune to make up for his unhappy childhood. But now Elise had awakened an uneasy sense of conscience in him. Finally he decided to give up on trying to sleep.

"Maybe a walk will help me out," he thought. Soon he was striding down the city streets. When he was thoroughly worn out, Victor wearily turned toward a well-lit restaurant.

"Hullo!" said a familiar voice from a table near the door. He recognized Frank Ward, a man who had an office in the same building as he did.

"Are you having trouble sleeping, too, old fellow?" laughed Ward.

"Yes," said Victor, taking a seat at the table. "I believe I'm getting a case of nerves. I think I need toning up."

"Well, you'd have been toned up if you were here just a few minutes ago," Ward laughed.

"What was it?" asked Victor.

"Why—a fellow came in here, a nice sort of fellow, apparently. He wanted to have supper. Well, when they wouldn't serve him, he wanted to fight everyone in sight. It was quite exciting for a time."

"Why wouldn't the waiter serve him?" Victor tried to make his tone casual. But he felt his voice shaking.

"Why? Why—he was black, you see,"

Ward answered with a wink.

"Well, what of it?" demanded Grabert fiercely. "Wasn't he quiet, well-dressed, polite? Didn't he have enough money to pay for his meal?"

"My dear fellow!" Ward laughed. "I believe you are losing your mind. You *do* need toning up—or something. Would you—could you—serve a colored man?"

"Oh, pshaw," Grabert broke in. "You may be right. Perhaps I *am* losing my mind. Really, Ward, I need something to make me sleep. My head aches."

Ward was at once full of sympathy and advice. But as soon as he could, Victor left the restaurant.

"That was a mistake," he said to himself. "What will I do next?" His remark had burst from his lips before he knew it. What had come over him? At home he got ready for bed.

"I have to be careful," he muttered. "If necessary, I must go to the other extreme." Suddenly he faced the mirror.

"If they knew, you wouldn't fare any better than the rest," he told himself. "You poor wretch—*what are you?*"

Then he thought of Elise and smiled. He loved her—even though he hated the traditions she represented. Deep down he felt a blind fury that drove him to take vengeance on those traditions. But at the same time, a cowardly fear cried out in him. He made up his mind. *At any cost* he must keep his position in the world—and in Elise's eyes.

* * *

Mrs. Grabert was delighted that her old school friend was visiting. The two women had already spent hours laughing about their school days and talking about their little ones.

"But Elise, I think it so strange you don't have a mammy for Baby Vannier," Mrs. Allen said.

"I think so too, Adelaide," sighed Mrs. Grabert. "I cried and cried for my old mammy. But Victor was firm about it. He doesn't like blacks, you know. He thinks old mammies just frighten children, and ruin their childhood. I don't see how he could say that, do you?"

"I truly don't," Mrs. Allen said. "We were all looked after by *our* mammies. I think they are the best kinds of nurses."

"And Victor won't have any black servants either. Not here or at the office," Mrs. Grabert said. "He says they're shiftless and worthless."

Mrs. Allen stared hard at the ceiling. "Oh, well, men don't know everything," she said. "One of these days Victor may come around to our way of thinking."

It was late that evening when the lawyer came in for dinner. For some reason he seemed nervous and restless. Elise glanced into his eyes. She knew right away that something must have disturbed him that day. But she asked no questions. She knew he would tell her when the time was right.

In their room that night, he stared into the open fire. Then he wearily passed his hand over his forehead.

"I'm afraid I had a rather . . . unpleasant experience today," he began.

"Yes?" she said.

"Pavageau, again."

At the name, Elise turned quickly. "I can't understand, Victor. Why must you have dealings with that man? I simply wouldn't associate with him."

"Well, I don't," Victor laughed. "It's only business that throws us together."

She came to his side. "Victor," she began, "won't you give up politics—for me? You've changed so. Why, Baby and I won't even know you after a while!"

"You mustn't blame the politics, darling," he said. "I don't think that's it. Maybe it's just that men change as they grow older. Don't you think so?"

"No, I don't," she replied angrily. "Why do you go on and on with this struggle? Why must you always be mixed up with such awful people, anyhow?"

"I don't know," he said wearily.

In truth, he did not know. After his marriage to Elise he had gone on making one success after another. He had a very high position in the opinion of the world. But this very fact made him tremble. *Something might come out.* How could he stand it if that happened? The crush of public opinion would overwhelm him.

"But nothing *will* come out," he would always say to himself. "Where could it come from?" And so he would comfort himself for the time being.

Pavageau was the thorn in his side. Pavageau was a coolheaded lawyer. His steely eyes were widely set in a grim brown face. Victor had first met him in the courtroom. Pavageau lost his case to Grabert, of course. But he had fought his fight with a great skill that commanded Victor's respect.

He wanted to go to Pavageau and shake his hand. He wanted to say that

he was proud of him. But he dared not.
Pavageau and the rest of the world might
misunderstand. Or would they?

Secretly, Victor admired the man. He
respected and liked him. Because of this,
however, he was always ready to fight
him. He fought him so bitterly that
Pavageau had become his enemy. Elise
had noticed it. She now traced her
husband's fits of depression to this one
source.

Meanwhile, Grabert's son was growing
up. He was a handsome lad, with his
parents' physical beauty. He also had a
strength and force of character that was
his alone. In him, Grabert had fulfilled
all his own longings. The boy had family
traditions and a social position that
belonged to him from birth. He had the
right to hold up his head without an
unknown fear gripping his heart. Victor
had bought and paid for his son's
freedom and happiness. The price may
have been his heart's blood—but he had

been more than willing to pay it.

* * *

One Saturday his son asked to go along to court with his father. Victor Grabert was now a judge.

"There is nothing that would interest you today, my son," Victor said. "But you may come if you like."

The first case that day involved a troublesome old woman. She was represented by Pavageau. His client, a black woman, had a fair-skinned grandchild who attended a school for white children. When the boy's true story was discovered, the woman was told to take the child out. Rather than do that, however, she brought the matter to court. Of course, she lost her case—for the law was very clear on the matter.

The judge was angry that his time should have been wasted on such a simple thing. "I don't see why these people want to force their children into the white schools," he declared. "There should be a strict inspection to prevent it. All the suspected children should be made to go where they belong."

Pavageau, too, was annoyed that day. He met Grabert's cold eyes with a penetrating stare of his own. "Perhaps Your Honor would like to set the example. Perhaps you should take *your* son from the white schools," he said.

There was instant silence in the courtroom. Every eye turned on the judge. Grabert sat still with flushed face and fear-stricken eyes. A minute passed. Why did he not speak? Pavageau should be punished for this insult. Yet he did nothing. Was His Honor ill? Or did he merely hold the man in too much contempt to notice his rude remark?

Finally Grabert spoke. "My son— does—not—attend the public schools."

Someone laughed. The atmosphere lightened at once. Clearly Pavageau was an idiot. His Honor was too much of a gentleman to notice him. Grabert continued calmly. "The gentleman doubtless intended a little joke. But this is a courtroom. I shall have to fine him for contempt of court."

"As you will," replied Pavageau. But he flashed a look of triumph at Grabert. His Honor's eyes dropped beneath it.

Grabert's son wondered about it. "What did that man mean, father? He said you should take me out of school," young Vannier said on their way home.

"He was angry, my son, because he had lost his case. When a man is angry he is likely to say silly things. By the way, I hope you won't say anything to your mother about what happened today. It would only annoy her."

The public forgot the incident as soon as it was over. But it was forever stamped on Grabert's memory. Again and again he tossed on a sleepless bed. Over and over he saw the cold flash of Pavageau's dark eyes and heard his soft-spoken

accusation. *How did the man know?*
Where had he gotten his information?

Sometimes Victor thought that Elise,
even, was suspecting him. When he
opened court each morning, it seemed
that every eye looked on him in scorn.

Finally he could stand it no longer. He
went to Pavageau's office. Nervously
mopping his forehead, he took the chair
Pavageau offered him. Then with a
sudden, almost brutal directness, he
turned on the lawyer.

"See here, what did you mean by that
remark you made about my son in court
the other day?"

"I meant just what I said," was
Pavageau's cool reply.

Grabert paused. "Well, why did you say
it?" he asked slowly.

"Because I was a fool. I should have
kept my mouth shut until another time.
Shouldn't I?"

"Pavageau," said Grabert softly, "let's
not play games. Where did you get your

information? You must tell me."

"Did you ever hear of a Madame Guichard of Hospital Street?" Pavageau asked.

Sweat broke out on the judge's brow. "Yes," he replied weakly. "Of course."

"Well, I am her nephew," Pavageau explained.

"And she?"

"—is dead. But she told me about you a few years ago. With pride, let me say. No one else knows."

Grabert sat dazed. He had forgotten about Madame Guichard.

"If—if—this were known to my wife, it would hurt her very much," he said thickly.

Pavageau looked up quickly. "It happens that I often have cases in your court. I am willing, if I lose fairly, to give up. But I don't like some of the decisions made against me. I don't like to lose because my opponent is of a different complexion than mine. Or because the decision against me would please a certain class of people. I only ask what I have never had from you—fair play."

"I understand," said Grabert.

As he walked out of the office, Victor admired Pavageau more than ever. Yet his admiration was mixed with a cold knowledge. *This man was the only person in the world who knew his secret.* The formless fear that had dogged his life now had a definite shape. At last he could lay his hands on it, and fight back. But with what weapons?

All he could do was back down from his position on certain questions. And what would be the result? Wouldn't suspicions be raised by this sudden change? Wouldn't people begin to question and to wonder? Would someone remember Pavageau's remark that morning? Maybe they would put two and two together. Maybe rumors would start flying. Victor's heart sickened at the very thought of it.

Then he threw back his head and laughed. Oh, what a glorious revenge he'd had on those little white village boys! How he'd made their whole race pay for all the insults they had given his own people—the very people he had denied!

Victor had gotten a diploma from one of the best white colleges. He had broken down the barriers of their social world. He had taken the highest possible position among them. He had copied their own ways, too. He had shown them that he could also hate this inferior race they hated—even if it was his own. He had taken for his wife the best woman among them. And she had borne him a fine son. Ha! What a joke on them all.

Victor had not forgotten the black boys, either. They had stoned him too, and he had lived to spurn them. He had looked down on them. He had crushed them every day from his seat on the bench. Truly, his life had not been wasted.

Victor had lived 49 years now. And the peak of his power was not yet reached. There was much more to be done. He owed it to Elise and the boy. For their sake he must go on and on, keeping his tongue still.

His duty was clear. He would give in to Pavageau and suffer alone. Someday, perhaps, he would have a grandson. And that grandson would be able to point with pride to "My grandfather, the famous Judge Grabert!"

That night there was a banquet in Judge Grabert's honor. He was to be the featured speaker. As he stood up, he smiled at the eager faces looking up at him. Then the applause died away, and a hush fell over the room.

"What a sensation I could make now," he thought. He had only to open his mouth and cry out, "Fools! What do you know of the man you are honoring? I am one of the hated ones. Yes, I'm black—do you hear, *black*!" If he were alone in the world, he would do it—just to see their horror and wonder. What could they do? Perhaps they would take away his office. But his wealth, and his successes, and his learning, they could not touch. Well, he must begin his speech. And he must think of Elise and the boy.

"Mr. Chairman," he began. But then Victor paused. How odd! In the place of the chairman sat Grandmere Grabert! She was looking at him sternly. He knew what she expected. She was waiting for him to give an account of his life since she had kissed him good-bye. He was surprised, and not a little annoyed.

"Mr. Chairman," he said again. But he could not go on. What was the use of addressing Grandmere that way? She would not understand him. He would call her Grandmere, of course.

"Grandmere," he said softly, "you don't understand—" And then he sat down in his chair again. He was angrily pointing his finger at her because no other words would come out of his mouth. They stuck in his throat. Then he choked and beat the air with his hands. Two men rushed over to him with water and fans. But Victor fought them away wildly.

Weren't they the boys with the stones? Wouldn't they laugh at him for wanting to play with them? Yes, he knew who they were. He would run away to Grandmere. She would comfort him. So he got up, stumbling and shrieking. Beating the boys back, he ran the length of the hall. Then he fell across the threshold of the door. He died as he hit the floor.

Victor's secret died with him—for he had been right about Pavageau's character. His enemy's lips remained sealed forever.

Thinking About
the Stories

Hope Deferred

1. Is there a hero in this story? A villain? Who are they? What did these characters do or say to form your opinion?

2. Think about the times in which this story is set. What circumstances in the story do not exist today? What legal and ethical standards apply now that didn't then?

3. Many stories are meant to teach a lesson of some kind. Is the author trying to make a point in this story? What is it?

Titee

1. Good writing always has an effect on the reader. How did you feel when you finished reading this story? Were you surprised, horrified, amused, sad, touched, or inspired? What elements in the story made you feel that way?

2. Is there a character in this story who makes you think of yourself or someone you know? What did the character say or do to make you think that?

3. Interesting story plots often have unexpected twists and turns. What surprises did you find in this story?

The Stones of the Village

1. What period of time is covered in this story—an hour, a week, several years? What role, if any, does time play in the story?

2. Some stories are packed with action. In other stories, they key events take place in the minds of the characters. Is this story told more through the characters' thoughts and feelings? Or is it told more through their outward actions?

3. Compare and contrast Victor Grabert to his rival, Pavageau. How are they different from or similar to each other? What is the source of their conflict? Do they eventually resolve their differences? How?